Touching

Copyright © 1980, Raintree Publishers Inc.

Library of Congress Number: 79-28393

    4 5 6 7 8 9 0 88 87 86 85 84

Printed in the United States of America.

Library of Congress Cataloging in Publication Data

Allington, Richard L
  Touching.

  (Beginning to learn about)
  SUMMARY: Explores the touch and feel of objects
that are scratchy, warm, squishy, bumpy, etc.
Also includes activities based on the material
presented.
  1. Touch — Juvenile literature. [1. Touch]
I. Cowles, Kathleen, joint author. II. Miyake,
Yoshi. III. Title. IV. Series.
QP451.A44   152.1'82   79-28393
ISBN 0-8172-1294-9 lib. bdg.

Richard L. Allington is Associate Professor, Department of Reading,
State University of New York at Albany.
Kathleen Cowles is the author of several picture books.

BEGINNING TO LEARN ABOUT

TOUCHING

BY RICHARD L. ALLINGTON, PH.D., • AND KATHLEEN COWLES

ILLUSTRATED BY YOSHI MIYAKE

Raintree Childrens Books • Milwaukee • Toronto • Melbourne • London

I was a baby when I first started touching.
At first I felt only soft things.
Now I touch and feel new things every day.

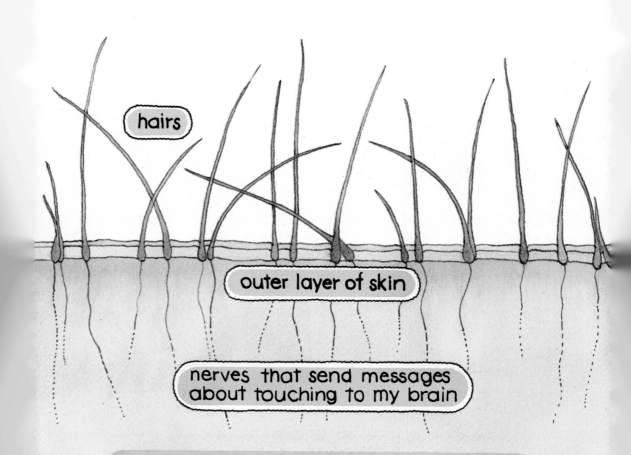

hairs

outer layer of skin

nerves that send messages
about touching to my brain

My skin tells me about what I touch.

I touch things with my feet—indoors . . .

5

dirt

hot sidewalk

stones

grass

. . . and outdoors.
Which places do you like to walk in your
bare feet? Which places hurt your feet?

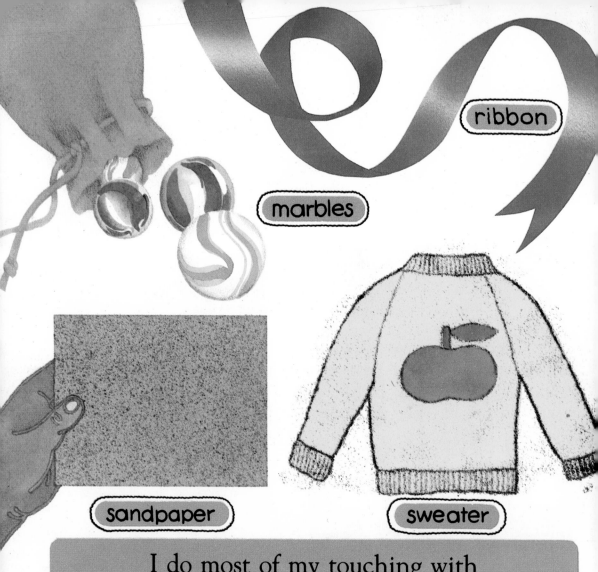

ribbon

marbles

sandpaper

sweater

I do most of my touching with my hands. Some things feel scratchy, and some feel smooth. Which of these things feel scratchy to you? Which feel smooth?

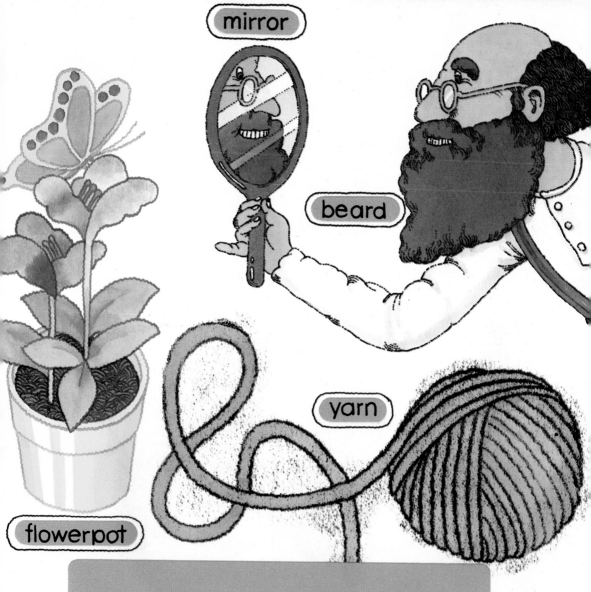

mirror

beard

yarn

flowerpot

Can you find other things around you
that feel scratchy or smooth?

hot chocolate

lamp

fish tank

Which of these things feel cool to you?
Which feel warm?

monkey bars

doorknob

coins

wet clothes

Can you find other things around you that feel cool or warm?

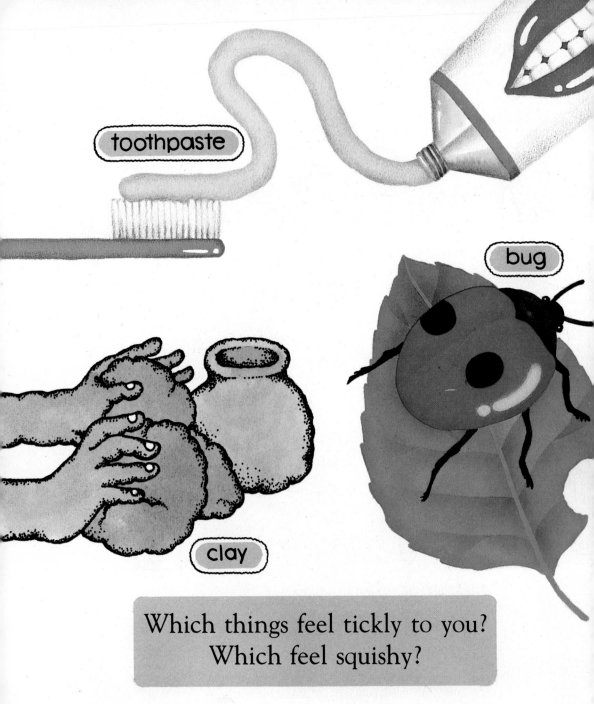

toothpaste

bug

clay

Which things feel tickly to you?
Which feel squishy?

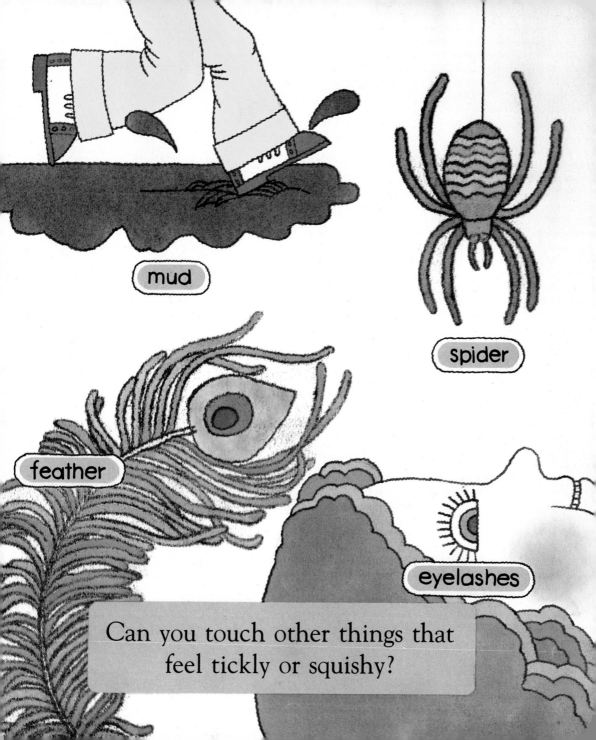

mud

spider

feather

eyelashes

Can you touch other things that feel tickly or squishy?

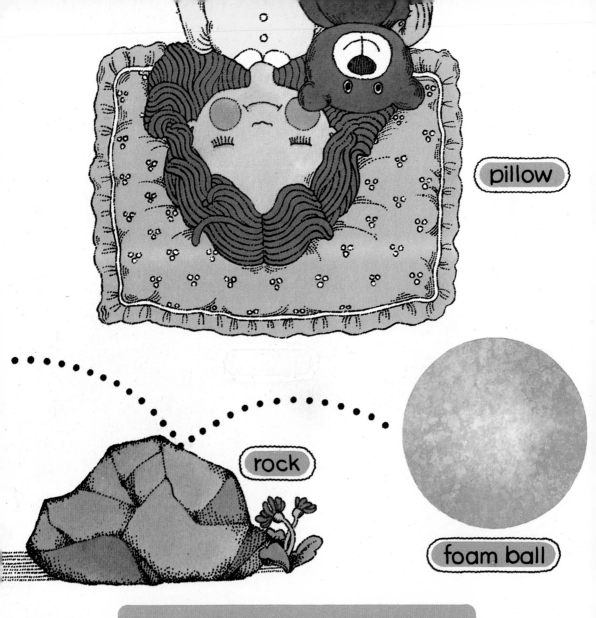

pillow

rock

foam ball

Which things feel solid to you?
Which feel spongy?

14

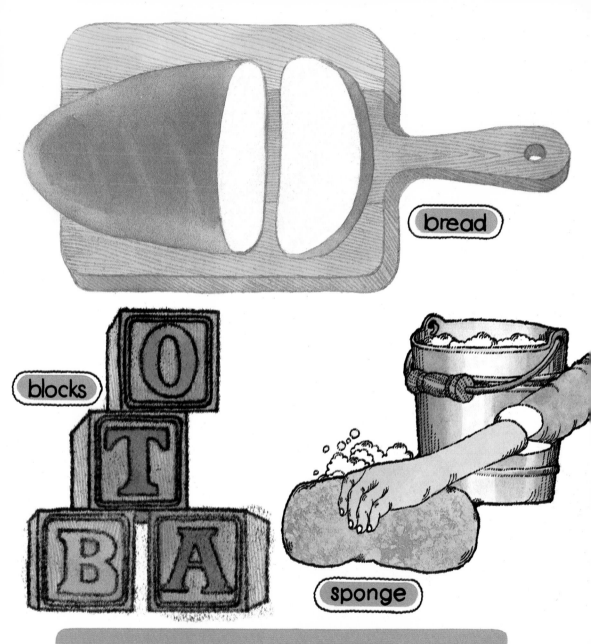

bread

blocks

sponge

What other things feel solid or spongy?

rain

shampoo

worms

Which things feel wet to you?
Which things feel dry?

seeds

seashell

blue jeans

balloon

kitten

wood

ball

Which things feel hard to you?
Which things feel soft?

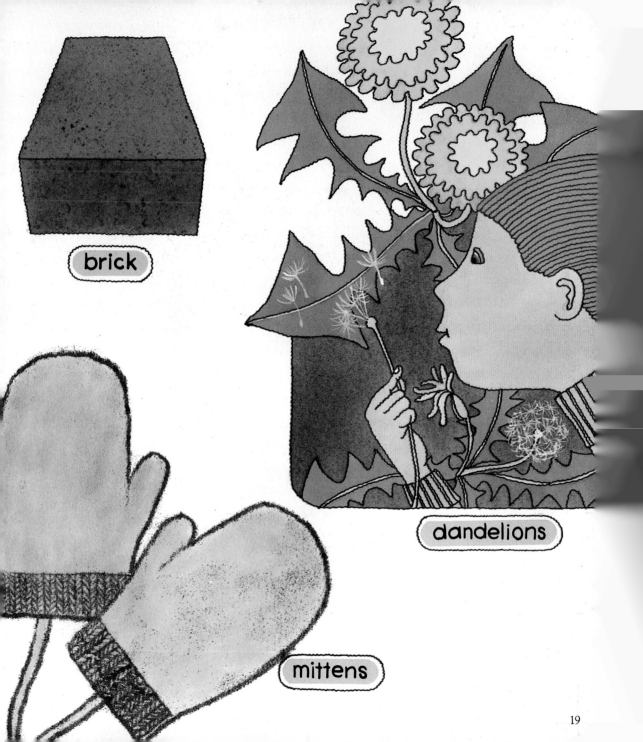

brick

dandelions

mittens

pumpkin

notebook

3 + (

tabletop

Which things feel bumpy to you?
Which things feel flat?

pan

tire

bottle caps

zipper

trash can

tape

slippers

paste

gum

snake

Which things feel sticky?
Which things feel fuzzy?
Which things feel slippery?

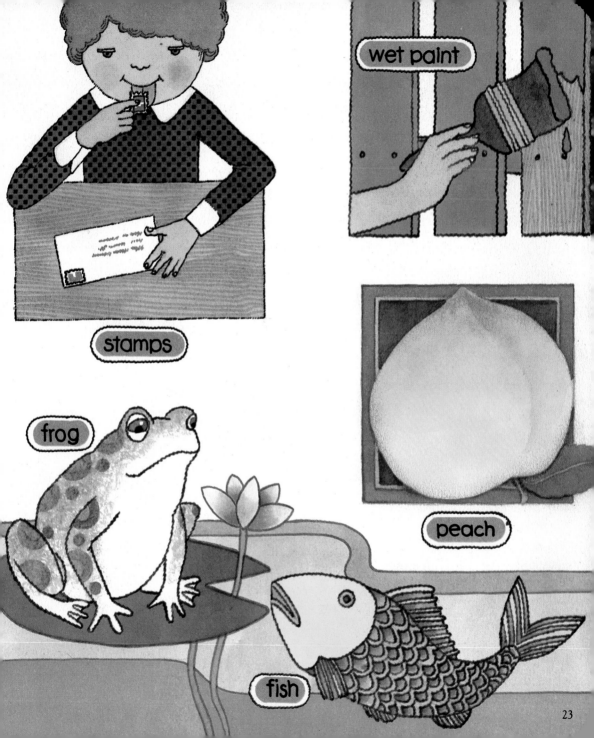

wet paint

stamps

frog

peach

fish

23

pine tree

light bulb

hairbrush

dog

Which things feel furry?
Which things feel prickly?

egg

broom

toothbrush

teddy bear

bubbles

Which things feel as if
they would break easily?

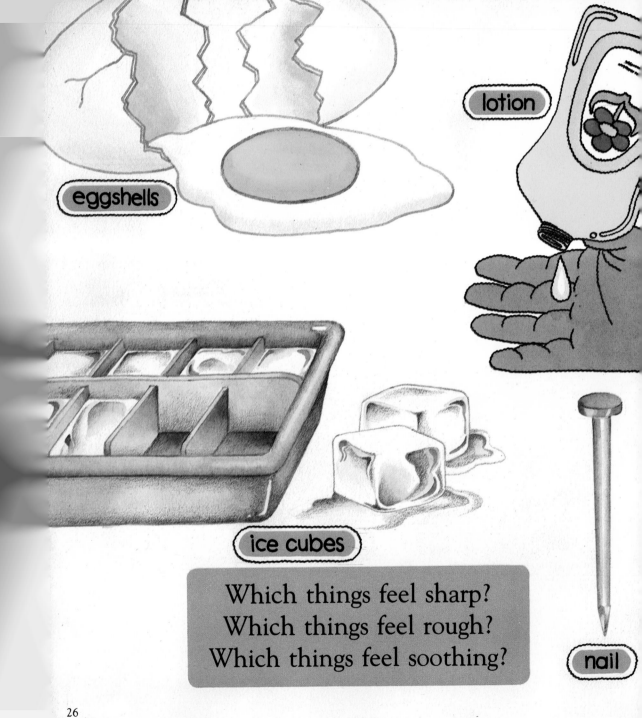

eggshells

lotion

ice cubes

nail

Which things feel sharp?
Which things feel rough?
Which things feel soothing?

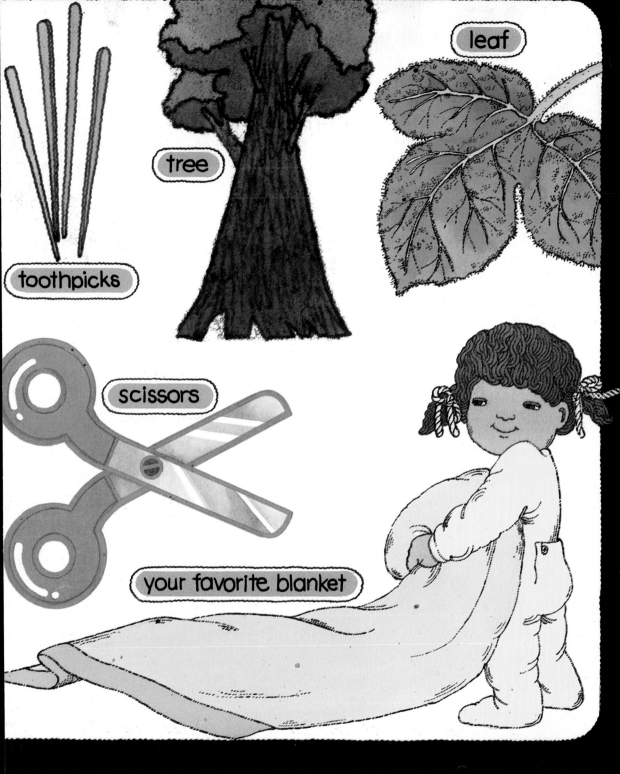

toothpicks

tree

leaf

scissors

your favorite blanket

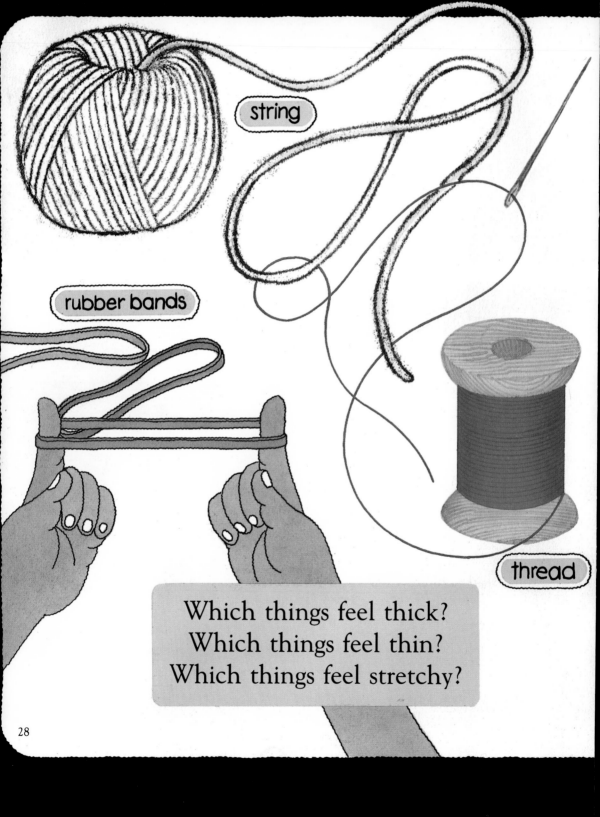

string

rubber bands

thread

Which things feel thick?
Which things feel thin?
Which things feel stretchy?

28

straw

telephone cord

your hair

spoon

fork

record

ring

buttons

Which things feel curved?
Which things feel pointed?
Which things feel grooved?

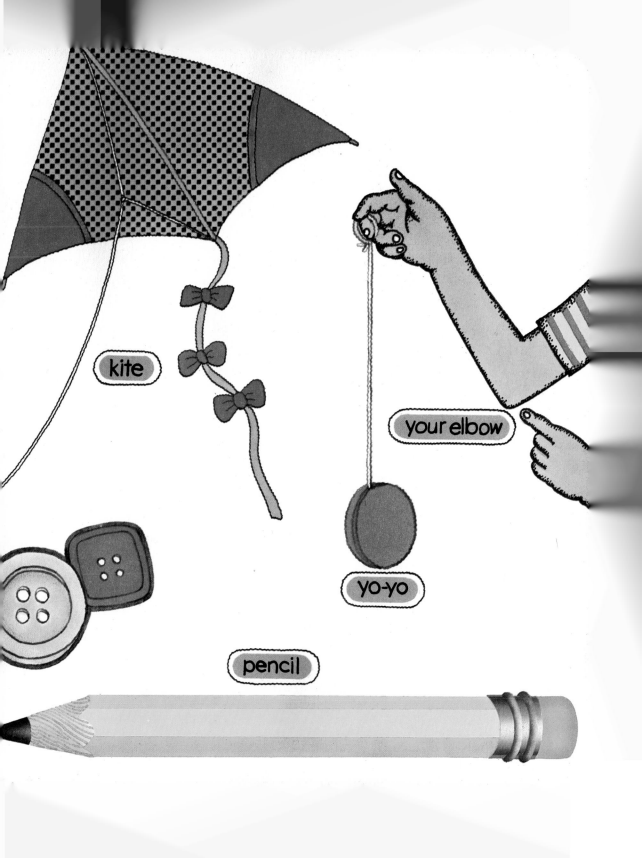

kite

your elbow

yo-yo

pencil

Ask someone to gather some of the things shown in this book. Shut your eyes. Then have the other person hand you the things. Touch them, one by one. Can you tell what each one is?
How can you tell?

What would it be like to touch these things:

clouds

moon

snow on the North Pole

stars

bottom of the ocean

What words would you use to tell about them?

You can make your own book about touching. Take several pieces of heavy paper such as construction paper, cardboard, or old playing cards. On each piece, paste something small and fun to touch. You might use rice or macaroni, beans, old zipper, leaves, bottle caps, piece of velvet or other kind of fabric, buttons, coins, piece of sandpaper, string or ribbon, toothpicks. Can you make up a story to go with the things in your book about touching?